OUR LITTLE CORINTHIAN COUSIN OF LONG AGO

This edition published 2026
by Living Book Press

ISBN: 978-1-76183-130-0 (hardcover)
         978-1-76183-129-4 (softcover)

First published in 1937.

A catalogue record for this book is available from the National Library of Australia

Our Little Corinthian Cousin of Long Ago

by

Phyllis Ayer Sowers

The Chariot Race

CONTENTS

FOREWORD

THIS is not meant as a history. The author will be content if she has given a clear and realistic picture of life in those days somewhere between 500 and 400 B.C. when Greece was in its glory, and she hopes to interest young readers in some of the splendor and culture of those days whose influence may be recognized even in modern times.

P.A.S.

CHAPTER I

TIMON OF CORINTH

"THERE is no other city so rich and gay as Corinth," declared Timon proudly. "If you argued all day and all night you could not make me think or say that any other place is half so fine!"

He was talking to a boy from Athens, a trader's son about his own age, who had just come in on a ship.

Athens and Corinth were both great cities in Greece, but in those ancient times the large cities were like separate states and there was much rivalry between them. In fact, Timon felt as though his own city of Corinth were a separate country, and loved it dearly, as did all the Corinthians.

The boy from Athens looked at Timon's muscular arms and strong brown legs which showed below his workman's tunic, and decided not to argue any more. If they should quarrel, he was sure Timon would win, so the rich young Athenian picked up his embroidered cloak and walked away without another word.

Timon looked at the sun, hanging low over the sea,

and hastily picked up a big bundle he had been carrying when he met the trader's son. "I must get back to the shop by lamplight time or old Ambrose will be very angry and perhaps no longer let me work for him. But how I wish I were rich enough so I could do as I like with my time!"

With a parting look at the many ships from different countries which lay in the harbor—and finest of all, the two Corinthian war galleys guarding the entrance—he turned and hurried up the hilly road.

The road from the harbor was bordered by two long city walls and Timon went through a stately gateway, on past the marketplace, now quiet and deserted, and on along the shadowy road where many other workers were hurrying homeward.

Part way up the hill, Timon paused, shifted his bundle onto the other shoulder and looked up at the beautiful citadel called the Acro-Corinthus, which guarded the city, and the splendid temple, its tall columns gleaming in the last rays of the sun. Though he had seen them many times before, Timon never grew tired of such a fine sight.

An old man leaning on a knotty stick stopped and smiled at him. "I see you like beautiful things, boy," he said. "That is the true spirit of a Grecian. Man has been

"I See You Like Beautiful Things, Boy"

able to make many beautiful things by studying nature—and nature is always beautiful!"

"He must be a poet or a philosopher," thought Timon with interest. You might meet all kinds of learned and interesting people on the streets of Corinth.

The old man went on speaking. "Now look over there at the peak of sacred Mt. Parnassus still shining with light. I suppose you know it is the home of the Delphic oracle who can foretell the future; and there also is the cave of the muses, who inspire the hearts of men with art and music; and the famous fountain of Castalia. If you drink from that you will be able to write fine poetry!"

"I have heard of these wonders, good sir," said Timon, "but I don't suppose I can ever go to Mt. Parnassus or travel beyond the city of Corinth, for I am poor!"

"Who knows?" answered the old man, patting Timon on one sturdy shoulder. "Go your way, boy, but don't forget that to the young, all doors may open!"

As Timon walked on, thinking of these words, he felt as though his heavy bundle had grown lighter. It was nice to be young and healthy, even if one were poor.

When he was a baby, Timon's father was a wealthy merchant and the family had many comforts and riches—but that was too long ago for him to remember. His father's ship had been lost at sea and his mother then had to work hard for food and clothes. And now Timon was an orphan and had to earn his living as best he could.

The road now dipped down into the dusty, crowded streets of the city, where one house elbowed up close to another and there were many shops. Timon was jostled and bumped by all kinds of people. There were no sidewalks nor street lights in this ancient city, and no clocks to tell time—but men knew the day was nearly over and were hurrying home.

"Out of the way!" shouted a voice, and Timon heard the sound of wheels and of horses' pounding hoofs. A chariot came down the narrow street, driven by a tall man who stood holding the reins. Beside him stood a boy about the age of Timon, but dressed in a fine linen cloak, high-laced sandals ornamented with silver, and with curly hair cut short but carefully arranged in the latest style of that day.

Timon stared a little, even as he tried to step back out of the way, but the proud driver was not satisfied. "Out of the way, slave!" he cried, and leaning sideways gave Timon a push with the handle of his whip. Timon lost his balance and fell down in the dirty street, but jumped to his feet at once, frowning angrily.

The boy in the chariot looked around and grinned a little at the sight of Timon brushing dust from his tousled hair, but was a little sorry for him and tossed him a coin of money as they drove on.

On one side of the coin was a picture of Pegasus, the winged horse of mythology stories, and Timon knew it was enough money to buy him a pair of sandals which he needed very much—for his feet were bare—but he was too angry to keep it and instead threw it right back and muttered: "If I ever see that boy again, I'll tell him what I think of him! Even his charioteer was better dressed than I!" And feeling the world was not treating him very well, he hurried on.

Timon looked up at the houses, most of them two stories high. There were no windows on the first floor looking toward the street, but the upper story was built out over it a little, and there he could see the lights of lamps beginning to flicker—and quickened his steps still more.

From the curtained window of one large house, Timon saw a pretty little girl and a woman looking out. As the women of the best families hardly ever went out of the home, it was a change for them to watch what went on in the street, and Timon thought, "I wouldn't want to be even a rich girl."

Just to see what they would do, he waved his hand,

and the little girl giggled and, calling, "Here is something for you, boy," tossed a small toy out the window.

The nurse slapped her and pulled her back into the room, but Timon picked up the toy and saw that it was a little silver wheel on a linen cord. When he jerked the string, the wheel would wind up and down it. Even grown women liked to amuse themselves with such toys in Greece, and as Timon whirled the pretty thing, he felt more cheerful.

When at last he reached the shop entrance, there was old Ambrose the overseer, with his grizzled white beard, peering out into the dusky street. "I thought perhaps you had decided to go to Egypt," he said angrily. "What makes you so late, worthless boy? Oh, I see you have been buying a toy. Get inside with the load of clay before I beat you!"

Timon hastily thrust the little wheel into his belt and began helping the other workers to sweep the shop, put away the tools, and cover half-finished pieces of pottery they had been making with damp cloths. There really wasn't much he could say in excuse for having taken so much time.

As soon as it was entirely dark, the workshop was locked and the men allowed to go home, and in a few

"Here Is Something For You, Boy"

swift strides, Timon had reached the blacksmith's shop where he lived.

"Good evening, Cosimo," he called cheerfully.

It wasn't much of a place to call home, but the orphan boy was very grateful to be allowed to live there.

Cosimo waved a knotty fist in greeting. He was sitting on a stool in the light of the forge, cleaning some fish to eat, and the firelight on his great beard and shining body made Timon think of old Greek stories of Vulcan, god of fire, who was supposed to make all the armor for the gods of Olympus and to have made the chariot of the sun. It was even said that Vulcan made himself automatic hand-maidens out of gold and silver to help him, and that he had workshops under the volcanoes which sometimes spouted out fire from his mighty forges! (Our word volcano comes from Vulcan.)

But Cosimo was dressed only in a short leather apron which wrapped around his waist and fastened in front, and his longish curly hair was held in place by a fillet of leather.

"Come and sit by the forge, my young friend," he said. "Even in this gentle climate of Corinth the evening air is chilly. Tell me the adventures of the day."

"It has not been a very lucky day for me," said Timon gloomily. "Ambrose, the overseer, treats me only a little better than he does the slaves and I am afraid will soon get tired of letting me work there. Do you think it wrong, Cosimo, for me to like to linger and watch the shipping and all the busy life of fair Corinth? When I am in the shop I work fast and do my best!"

"Of course you do, Timon," agreed the smith, giving him a hearty slap on the back. "I think you are too good a craftsman for him to send you away! You have learned well how to handle a paint brush or engraving tool after the artists have drawn a picture on a clay vase!" Cosimo tossed his fish onto a pan and went on cheerfully:

"I remember the first time I saw you. Then you were only a thin little boy helping the cleaners whiten the soiled clothes of wealthy people, but I liked you and brought you here to live, and now you work in the rich trader's factory where they make fine pottery to send on ships to far parts of the world. Already I am proud of you!"

By this time, Timon felt happy and encouraged. "I hope the little work I do for you will help someday to make you wealthy," he said, laughing. "And when I become a famous athlete, since I have no father alive, I shall name you, along with the city of Corinth, to share the honors!"

Cosimo laughed. "I am afraid you are looking too far ahead, my boy, but if that day ever comes, I shall be glad indeed. Come now and eat."

As soon as they had finished their simple meal of fish

and a kind of porridge flavored with peppers and garlic—which the people of the south liked as well in those days as in these—Timon jumped to his feet saying: "Now for a little exercise to strengthen my muscles. Is there anything I can make for you, Cosimo?"

"Take yonder bar and flatten it. Perhaps later I may use it to make a spear or a shield or to mend that chariot wheel." He pointed to one which stood against the wall.

After a hard day's work, Cosimo himself was glad enough to lean back against the wall of sun-dried bricks and do nothing, while Timon drew his tunic up under his belt so it would be still shorter and let the sleeve of it fall off his right shoulder, as many workmen did, the better to use his right arm. For a while, there was no sound but the ring of the heavy iron hammer against the red-hot bar.

But before long, some visitors strolled in from the street, for the sea-air at night was a little chilly and the forge-fire looked comfortable. Some of these men were rich young idlers with nothing much to do. They scorned most kinds of work, but did not look down upon the work of a powerful blacksmith. There were also two young officers from the city fortress and an old soldier named Ajax.

Of all the callers who sometimes dropped in, Timon liked best to listen to the tales of the old soldier, and fortunately his work was done, so he laid down the hammer and said: "Tell us some of the adventures you had when you were young, good Ajax?"

The old man sat down on the three-legged stool which Cosimo pushed forward, and the others made themselves comfortable, and with his keen eyes shining like those of the eagle for which he was named, he told tales of war—of battering-rams carried against the enemy cities; fighting-towers full of brave archers, of whom needless to say Ajax had been one (for he seemed to have been the hero in every one of his stories). He told how they had piled mounds of earth secretly at night against some foreign city's walls and how Ajax had been among the first of the soldiers to scramble over and win the praise of his mighty general.

Most exciting of all was the story of the tremendous sea-battle of Salamis, which had saved the Greek world from the conquering Persian hosts and their King Xerxes.

"I doubt if he is old enough to have fought at Salamis," Cosimo whispered to Timon, "but anyway it is a good story!"

"Ay, it was a goodly fight," the old man was saying. "The Greek fleet, which numbered three hundred and seventy-eight great galleys, had cornered the Persian ships in the narrow waters near the enemy island of Salamis.

"Xerxes, the Persian king, sat upon a lofty throne built on a mountain-side, watching it all and wearing his tall golden crown. He was shaded by fine purple tents and surrounded by generals in shining armor, but on the sea was galley against galley, ramming each other, ripping off each other's great oars, while the air was full of flying arrows.

"Many Persian galleys broke to pieces, others escaped around the headland, and in the sea were many men—the Greeks, all good swimmers like young Timon here, but the Persians fared less well, and many drowned. Of all the Greek fighters from the many states, the Corinthians were the bravest!"

"Of course," murmured all the patriotic listeners, though this wasn't true, for the people called the "Athentians" had been judged to have first place for victory and given three golden stars on a mast in the sacred shrine at Delphi, and golden tablets were placed on the altar at Corinth.

Prizes were to be given to the two bravest men, and every captain was allowed to write down two names, one for first and one for second place. But each captain put his own name first and that of a hero named Themistocles, the second. So no prize could be given after all, for no one could decide who was really first.

"They should have chosen me," old Ajax chuckled.

One of the young officers laughed and said teasingly,

"Now tell us about the time you fought against the hero Hector and the men in the Trojan Wooden Horse!"

"And did you sail with brave Ulysses (sometimes called Odysseus) on his adventures?" asked another young man.

The old soldier grinned and nodded. He knew they were only joking, for these were heroes of ancient Greek stories and legends told by the Greek poet Homer in his books the 'Iliad' and the 'Odyssey', about times so long ago that not even the oldest man on earth could remember them, though the Greeks liked to think they were descendants of those heroes.

"Listen, masters," went on Ajax as heartily as ever. "I will tell you about the time our ship encountered the dreadful monsters Scylla and Charybdis, and how we were nearly wrecked on the rocks by the songs of the beautiful sirens."

"Enough!" cried one of the men, laughing and rising to his feet. "In a minute you will be telling us that Cosimo is really old Vulcan himself come down from Mt. Olympus! My friend and I must go on to a party, and good Cosimo and his apprentice lad are probably ready for sleep."

CHAPTER II

THE BOY IN THE CHARIOT

AFTER he had passed Timon on the street, the boy in the chariot began to feel sorry for what had happened. "Perhaps I ought to tell Gruno to drive more carefully," he thought. "It must be horrid to be poor and have the dust of the street all over one's only clothes, and he was a nice, strong-looking boy—but just the same he had no right to throw the money after me in that scornful way, and I'd like to tell him so!—Look, Gruno, at all those people standing around my father's house, looking at the door. Something interesting must be happening!"

The charioteer stopped the two great horses with a flourish and said, "Indeed yes, young master Arius. There is a large wreath of olive branches hung on the door. That means you have a new baby brother!"

"So it does!" cried Arius. "How happy my father and mother must be!" He jumped from the chariot and knocked loudly on the door. If the new baby had been a girl, they would have hung a wooden 'fillet' on the door so everybody would know. A 'fillet' which represented the bands Grecian people often wore about their hair.

A big black slave opened the door in a hurry. Even he was grinning happily and showed his white teeth, and a voice from upstairs called, "Hello, Arius. Come and see the new baby. It is so little and nice, almost like one of my dolls!"

"Hello, Althea," called the boy as he saw his little sister looking over the railing.

"Be careful not to make any noise," the black nurse-maid warned him when he reached the door of the nursery. This nurse was a slave, but she had been with the family for so many years that she had a good many rights and often told the children what to do.

Arius was allowed to look at the new baby, which was wrapped tightly in swaddling-clothes, yards and yards of cloth wound all about its little body and even binding its arms and legs. It looked like a big cocoon, and Arius could only see its wrinkled little red face.

"Run away now, Arius, and find your father," said the nurse. "He is in the living-room of the house, planning a party for his friends."

The nurse laid the baby in its hanging cradle, woven something like a basket. "Now will you tell me a story, please, Cora?" asked Althea, who had had an unusually dull day, for nobody had had time to think of anything much excepting the new baby.

"Shall I tell you about my old home in Ethiopia?" asked the woman, sitting down and taking the little girl on her lap.

"No, thank you, I know all about the monkeys and wild parrots and the traders who came and caught you and took you away on the ship," answered Althea, who had heard the story many times. "But you aren't sorry to be living here in Greece with us now, are you, Cora?"

"No, I am not sorry, for your father is a very kind master.—Now shall I tell you a fable of the old man named Aesop, who lived long ago? Some say he was a black slave like me, but so clever that nobody ever forgets his stories!"

"Yes, indeed. I'd like to hear the one about the fox and the grapes he said were sour because he couldn't reach them." Althea knew this story already, but liked the funny way Cora could tell it.

The people of Corinth, and indeed of all the world in those olden times, did not think it wrong to own slaves, and every rich person had a great many. Some had been captured in wars and were educated men and women, and others just poor people who were bought and sold like any other merchandise. But it sometimes happened that a master would let his slave make money at a trade until he had enough to buy his own freedom. Slaves did nearly all the work in ancient Corinth.

"Please tell me one more story," begged Althea when the fable was finished. "This time I would like an exciting one."

"Then I shall tell you the story of Phæton, whose father was Apollo, the ruler of the sun, who lives in the flaming palace of the sky. Each day, as you know, Apollo drives the Sun Chariot up and down the sky, giving light and warmth to all the earth!"

"Oh yes, sometimes I even see it start its journey, climbing up over Mt. Parnassus, or see him driving down under the sea at night," said Althea.

The Grecian people did not know there is only one God, but thought the many Gods of earth and sea and sky lived on the top of lofty Mt. Olympus in the part of Greece called Thessaly, and they liked to imagine life in things like trees and rocks, sun and water. Poetry and stories by the hundred grew up around these supposed characters—'nymphs' of the streams 'fauns of the woods' (gay goat-like little creatures), Pan the god of Nature who played on merry shepherd pipes, and many others. Althea and Cora thought the story of Apollo and Phæton had really happened once upon a time, and so Cora went on telling it.

Phæton lived upon the earth, but he was brave and ambitious and wanted very much to drive the sun-chariot at least once. He begged and begged until his father at last said yes. "But remember, Phæton," he warned him, "the horses are very strong and hard to manage. Be sure and keep them in the beaten course, for if you don't drive carefully, it will make a lot of trouble!"

"The sun-chariot, as you know, Althea, is made of gold and diamonds, so no one can even look at it when it is on the highest peak of the sky hill, but the father rubbed Phæton's face and arms with a magic ointment so he wouldn't be burned.

"The first part of the blue sky hill was so steep that the horses could hardly climb it even when fresh in the morning, but they soon noticed that the chariot was lighter than usual and tossed their fiery heads eagerly. Phæton felt very proud and happy as he saw the Moon leaping into her chariot and the Hours harnessing their horses to start on their sky journey one after another, but when he looked down from the high center of the sky, it almost took his breath away to see the earth so far below. Then they started down the sky, faster and faster! Phæton couldn't keep the horses in the road, and the Scorpion and Bear and other big star monsters were angry and threatened to hurt him.

"The chariot grew hotter and hotter. The clouds began to smoke, and the forests on mountain tops to burn, and snow to melt. Soon the whole earth was on fire, and the poor people of Lybia (Africa) turned black because they were all scorched!" Cora stopped her story to rub her own black cheek thoughtfully and wonder if it would feel any different to be white.

"Go on, Cora, please?" begged Althea.

"The Lybian desert was all dried up, as it is to this day, and Earth called to Jupitor, the king of all, to save her, so he threw his thunderbolts at Phæton, who fell from the chariot while the frightened horses ran home!"

The story was interrupted by a thin little cry from the baby's cradle, and Cora ran to its side. "Wait till you're a little older, wee baby," she said. "Then you too will want me to tell you some of the wonderful Greek stories!"

"I think I'm going to love him even better than I do my doll," said Althea, smiling down at the little brother, "but I should think he'd be uncomfortable tied up in all those tight clothes."

"Don't worry about that," answered Cora. "In four months they will take off the swaddling clothes, and then he will wear nothing more than a short jacket, and almost before you know it, will be playing about and perhaps pulling the small red cart Arius promised to make for him."

Althea began to plan some baby clothes for her doll. The doll was made of colored wax and had arms and legs which could be moved and clothes she could put on and off. Sometimes she dressed it in a long dress like a fine lady and sometimes in a short tunic like a Greek soldier. Arius had carved her a doll-sized shield and spear and little helmet. He was clever about making such things.

CHAPTER III

THE BIRTHDAY FESTIVAL

ABOUT a week later, Althea's mother said, "Ask Cora to put on your nicest white dress and bind your hair with red ribbons. We must go to the temple and take thank offerings because the baby is so well and strong!"

Greek religion was always happy, and there were no regular days for temple services, but the people went whenever they had some specially important prayers to make.

Today the baby's aunts and uncles and cousins went too, so it was a bright and pretty procession that went winding up the hilly road. Althea carried two white doves in a little cage, and Arius led a lamb around whose neck a wreath was hung, while its curly head was bound with a silken fillet as though it had been a person. The mother, Cora, and the baby, dressed in their finest, walked along shaded by a big flat-shaped parasol which was carried by a slave boy walking behind them. The parasol was made to project forward of the handle. After them came servants carrying great baskets of fruit and jugs of wine and olive-oil from the father's country estate, and others with perfumes and incense from Egypt.

The sun was shining brightly on the lovely graceful pillars and columns of the temple which men had built to show that they thought beauty and godliness always belong together. These temples were so much finer than the enormous temples of the Egyptians and other Oriental people, that even thousands of years later, people copy them and speak admiringly of the stately "Corinthian" columns and architecture.

Down below, as though in another world, the busy city was humming like a beehive, and in the two blue harbors where the water lay like shining silk almost surrounding Corinth, were ships which came from the uttermost parts of the world as it was then known.

"One of those ships belongs to me," said the father. "It is laden with pottery and wine to carry to distant Egypt far across the Mediterranean Sea, but from here I cannot tell which it is, for they all look like toys! See, there's a ship they are hauling across the land because they have to take it from one harbor to the other, and it is a hard way to move a ship. Too bad the wise ruler of Corinth, whose name was Periander, wasn't able to finish the canal across the isthmus as he wished to do."

The hundreds of slaves, hauling at ropes, looked from the hill like ants.

The Isthmus of Corinth, like a neck, joined the mainland of Greece to the great peninsula which in ancient times was called "Peloponnesus," and in these times, Morea.

"They are brave men who sail the little-known seas," said the father as he started to turn away, "but Corinthians have always been brave seamen!"

"It seems to me far braver to be a soldier!" said a boy named Lucien. "When I'm a man, I hope I can go to war."

"It is not the wisest of wishes," said his uncle. "Great trading-cities like Corinth should try to keep the peace with all countries. A few years ago we were at war with Athens, but now we are friendly enough, though I wish they did not have so many rival trading-ships upon the seas! Come, we must not stand talking longer. The others have reached the temple and I want to be the first to give money to the priests and priestesses in honor of the new baby!"

The interesting celebrations were not over when they reached home that evening, for people kept coming to the door or sending their slaves with presents for the baby and his mother.

"I think the nicest thing he has is this little necklace with all the silver ornaments," said Althea. They were amulets meant to bring the baby health and good fortune and skill—such things as a crescent moon, a tiny pig, a sword, a little pair of hands, and so on.

"The house looks so pretty with all the garlands of flowers, ivy, and olive branches," she added. "It is too bad he's so little he can't understand all these nice things!"

"But our mother can understand," said Arius fondly, "and I'm going to buy her a nice present myself when I have time. Tonight there will be a feast and even the women and girls will be invited, so you'd better look as pretty as you can, Althea, and I must hurry to bathe and dress myself in my finest!"

Usually the Grecian women did not eat with the men of the family.

Arius stood with his father when it was time to welcome the guests, many of whom brought slaves of their own to help serve them. As soon as they arrived, the newcomers took off their shoes and had their feet washed in bronze basins, so the dust of the street should not spoil the fine coverings on the father's dining couches. All the men lay down to eat, propping themselves up on one elbow amidst the embroidered cushions. Their wives sat on the foot of the couches, for women never lay down to eat, and Arius and Althea, like the other children, sat on low chairs nearby.

The slaves brought many three-legged tables, one for each guest, covered with good things to eat. There were no napkins or knives and forks, but all the food had been cut into small pieces in the kitchen and some-times they dipped into their plates with a piece of bread, hollowed into the shape of a spoon, while at the end of each course, a servant passed about towels and basins of water so the guests could wash their hands.

The meal ended with honey, fruits and little cakes in the shape of animals and human-beings. "And now it's time for us to go," the mother whispered to Althea. "Only the men will stay for the part of the meal called the 'symposium'!"

"Let Arius stay this once, if he wants to," said his father. "Now that I have a new born son, I feel as though Arius were almost a man," he explained laughingly to the guests.

Arius felt very pleased and proud as the servants carried away the small tables and brought others cov-ered with many sweets and bowls of weak wine mixed with water. "Only barbarians drink pure wine," said the father. By this he meant all those foreigners who could not speak Greek or understand its 'culture'. "Here slave, give my son one of the wreaths to wear upon his head." Even the big, bearded men wore wreaths of flowers at feasts.

Now with a burst of song and laughter, a troop of entertainers came running into the room. There were dancers in graceful swaying garments, and flute players and jolly jugglers; a man who shot a bow and arrow with his feet, and a girl who could swallow a sword and pull it out again, with a pleasant smile.

Another fellow made foolish jokes, telling one man who was bald to comb his hair, another who stammered to make a speech, and when he told Arius to comb his beard, they all laughed heartily.

But at length, to Arius' disappointment, his father ordered these entertainers to go away and then the guests held a contest to see who could play the zither best, recite poetry and guess at riddles, and Arius' head began to nod a little, though he tried to keep his eyes open and look as lively as anyone.

These friends of his father's were very intelligent men and they made a great many speeches and talked of things and people, whom Arius only knew a little about. Of Socrates and Plato the philosophers; of Phidias the famous sculptor; Pericles the wise ruler of Athens; Hippocrates the learned and good doctor, one of the first to teach that the health and welfare of people was much more important than to make money. All these, men who lived in Greece in those days and whose names and works will never be forgotten.

But Arius' father at length whispered to him, "You look sleepy and now you had better say good-night and go to bed!"

CHAPTER IV

GOING TO SCHOOL

"**W**AKE up young master," said the special slave who always had charge of Arius. "He who wants to be rich and wise and healthy, must not waste time in bed but rise early enough to see great Apollo drive his sun-chariot up the mountains of the sky!" He shook Arius gently, saying, "Quick master, your bath is ready and here are your clothes!"

Most Corinthians rose at sunrise and usually went to bed early. But after the late hours of the feast, Arius felt as though he had only been asleep a few minutes, and stifled a big yawn as he jumped out of bed and stepped into the flat bronze basin which served him as a bathtub.

The man slave now poured cool water over him, from a shining jug and in a moment Arius was wide awake and hurrying into his clothes. He was on time for an early breakfast with his father and together they went out on the street, followed by the black slave of Arius, a good man whom they both liked very much.

"Well Arius," said his father. "You look bright and

strong today. I hope you will do well in your school and gymnasium. Here is the barber-shop where I will have my beard trimmed, so good-bye."

The barber-shop was already full of rich customers, who called greetings to Arius' father. It was a place where wealthy and important men liked to gather early in the morning and exchange the latest news, for there were no newspapers in those days.

Another place men liked to go together, were the public baths which Arius passed, and he could see that the steam from the heated waterspouts was already rising on the cooler morning air.

But he and the slave walked fast until they reached the handsome gymnasium building and Arius waved to a group of boys he knew, who were also just arriving. One of them his cousin Lucien, whose father was a Magistrate in the city and who dressed very grandly. Even his slave wore gold earrings and fine linen clothes.

"Good morning, Lucien," said Arius. "I warrant I can beat you at jumping today."

"Well remember when we were throwing spears yesterday, it was I who won," answered Lucien. He always liked the military contests the best.

The boys bowed to the gymnasium master, a fine strong man wearing only a cloak and holding a switch.

All the boys admired him and he seldom used the switch, though sometimes when two boys were wrestling with all their strength they forgot it was all in sport and, growing angry, might forget some of the rules. Then they would feel the sting of the whip, as even Arius knew.

Though the boys took off all their clothes for the athletic training, they were soon covered with sweat and panting from the hard work.

"You won't get out of breath so quickly when you are in better training," the master said, throwing aside his cloak. "Now watch me throw the discus. This is the way to hold it to make it go the furthest." Without his cloak, the master looked like a bronze statue, his back as straight as a temple column. "Come now boys, take the weights and let me see how far you can jump today." Leaning down, he drew a line on the ground.

Arius looked at Lucien and Lucien looked at Arius and both of them had the same thought. "Today I will do better than he can!"

The Grecians held weights in each hand when jumping. If they held them correctly, the impetus would help them to go further. Arius was tall for his age and watched the master carefully and again he won the contest.

"Well done, Arius," said the master. "You have gone further than any boy today. Now let me see if you will do as well at boxing. It is not so important as jumping and wrestling, but will teach you to be quick of eye!"

Indeed professional boxing was a hard, cruel sport and Arius knew very well he would not like it. The boys' hands were bound with leather thongs, but men boxers often used gloves of heavy bull's hide, studded with knobs of hard metal.

After a short rest, the boys were getting ready for a wrestling match. "Ugh! Dirty sport," grumbled Lucien.

"Better not let the master hear you say that," warned Arius. "He says it is a fine and manly sport and that a strong, brown body is a sign of courage and shows one isn't just a slave who sits in a dim shop bending over a trade!"

"Then perhaps you'll like to be a real athlete and compete in the Olympic games!" said Lucien, who was pouring oil from a jug over his body, to make his muscles limber.

Arius, already greasy, was dusted with a special coating of earth from the gymnasium pit. After they finished wrestling this would be mixed with dirt from the ground and nothing but a thorough scraping, hot water, and lye would get them clean again.

"It would be grand to win undying fame for Corinth, by winning at the Olympic games," admitted Arius, "but true athletes have to spend years and years on special training and certain kinds of food and there isn't much time left to spend on book studies! My father wants me to learn the works of poets and philosophers as well as how to have a strong body!"

"If you boys waste so much breath in talking, you'll never be ready," said the master. "Get ready now and after the wrestling there will be a game of ball, which is more play than work!"

After a light lunch, the boys went to another building to "exercise their minds."

The teacher here was a thin man, with near-sighted, peering eyes. We should have said he needed eye-glasses, but no such thing was known in ancient Greece. He had spent much time bending over books even by the light of dim, flickering oil-lamps.

"But I suppose he knows nearly everything," whispered Arius.

"Take your places, boys," said the teacher, looking quickly about him. A row of sturdy slaves who had come with their young masters sat in the doorway, ready to keep order if necessary.

The teacher opened his big book, carefully written by hand on parchment paper. Only wealthy men could afford books in those days when everything had to be copied by hand.

The teacher sat on a stool while Arius stood before him and recited. "Now bring the abacus and do your sums," he said, closing the book.

Arius held the board, which was made with beads strung on wires. These represented numbers and could be pushed back and forth in rows under each other, so adding and subtracting was as easy as though he had used his fingers. It was all right there on the board and only needed to be counted.

Writing was practiced on wax-coated tablets. Arius used a stylus made of ivory to scratch on the wax, and when he made a mistake it could be smoothed out by using the flat end of the stylus.

The Greeks, who loved all beauty, thought that music was important for everyone. "Do not forget that music is good for the soul," said the teacher. "The great doctor Hippocrates uses it to cure people who have sick minds and sends his patients to the temple of Apollo, who is the God of music as well as of sunshine!"

In the music room was a statue of Apollo and many musical instruments, one of which was made from the shell of a tortoise and had horns of wood. This was called a lyre and was very popular. Poems were written to be chanted to the accompaniment of the lyre, and these were called lyric poems.

But about this time, Arius began to feel that he had had enough schooling for one day. His eyes kept wandering to the "water-clock" standing near the wall. This was a kind of a glass jar from which the water dripped slowly into a jug below, and when it was half empty, the boys knew the school hours were over.

Althea was waiting eagerly for her brother's return. She liked to hear the "adventures" of the day, as she called them, and liked to have him play with her.

"Shall we play on the see-saw, or roll our hoops with bells about the yard?" she asked.

Even quite big Grecian boys played at rolling hoops, but Arius said, "I think I've had enough exercise for a while. Shall we play a game of knuckle-bones?"

"All right. Sit here and I'll get them," she answered.

These playthings were made of the little round, nicely polished ankle-bones of a lamb (the rest of the lamb had been eaten for dinner, long ago). There were many ways to play the game, but Althea usually won.

"It's because I have so much time to practice," she said generously, skillfully tossing the little bones in the air and catching them on the back of her hand.

CHAPTER V
THE QUARREL

TIMON slept at the back of the blacksmith shop, where the eastern sunshine came in earliest. As soon as its warm fingers fell through the open window onto his face, he would open his eyes and spring to his feet. There was no time to waste if he didn't want to be late at the workshop.

"Good morning, Cosimo," he shouted, giving the burly blacksmith a friendly shove with his foot as he ran out into the street.

The morning air from the sea was sweet and fragrant, and the low sun made a long pale shadow of the column in the market-place, called the "shadow-marker." "It shows the day is new-born," thought Timon gaily, "and I am one of the first up to celebrate it."

Early in the morning he always felt as though anything nice might happen, and remembered the words of the old man on the road, "To the young all doors may open."

So, feeling very like a woodland faun on a painted vase, he leaped up the rise to the fountain in the market square and thrust his head under the head of the stone dolphin which spouted water from its open mouth. Sputtering and coughing, he next washed his dusty feet and legs and was finishing with his arms, when a voice said, "Hurry, boy. I cannot wait all day to carry water to my mistress!"

Timon stepped back and smiled at the Egyptian slave woman who stood with an empty jug balanced on a little mat on her head. Other women, some of them servants and others wives and daughters of poor shop-keepers, were coming up the hill carrying jars so as to get water for washing and cooking breakfast. Few people had running water in their homes in Corinth.

"Why do you look so happy?" asked the Egyptian, looking at him with her great black mysterious eyes. She made Timon feel as though she could know what he was thinking.

Timon was dripping, but the sunshine was warm already and soon he would be dry, clothes and all. He told the woman his idea. "Each new day seems to me like a shining writing tablet on which any brave deed or strange adventure may be scratched."

"So it is," she answered. "Would you like me to tell your fortune, boy? Have you anything with which to pay me?"

Timon thought of the little silver wheel-toy the girl

had tossed from the window and showed it to her. "This is all I have," he said. "I was going to exchange it for a pair of sandals."

"It will do," said the woman. "Now think what you want most in the world and do not talk!"

Timon had only one real ambition, and that was to be a famous athlete. Sometimes he pictured himself coming home in triumph from some distant city, riding in a chariot, dressed in purple (the favorite color of wealthy people and kings, for purple dye was beautiful and quite expensive); and he pictured the people running before him, shouting and making music; and perhaps they would tear down a part of the city wall as an honor, meant to show that a place which had such a brave and mighty citizen needed no walls to protect it. Timon had heard beside the forge in Cosimo's smithy, just such tales of real men who had become famous at the great games.

While he was thinking of these things, the woman put down her water-jar and, bending over, made a little heap of dust and began swirling her long, dark fingers slowly back and forth in it, staring into space.

"I see a tall boy—Yes, it is you—He is well-dressed and there is a great crowd.—They are cheering and a herald is blowing a trumpet…"

"Is it I? Am I the athlete?" demanded Timon eagerly.

But the Egyptian woman shook her head. "I cannot tell," she said solemnly, "but some change of fortune will come to you soon.—It is night. I see a moon with a band of clouds around it like a victor's fillet and three men—something which glitters—tomorrow night—Good or bad, your fortune will be what you make it yourself!"

"But how shall I know what to do?" asked Timon, whose voice shook with excitement. There were many 'soothsayers' in the marketplace during the busy hours, but never before had he had his fortune told.

The woman looked up and said, "Now I can see no more. I warned you not to talk," and she rose, shaking the dust from the edges of her skirt.

A little crowd of onlookers had gathered, and they laughed, thinking it a joke on Timon, who walked off as though in a dream. He scarcely noticed the awakening city. The market filling with buyers and sellers, the fishermen beginning to put out in their boats from shore, shouting to each other as they raced for the purple kelp-beds where the fish liked to loiter.

People were carrying their wares, and Timon came 'back to earth' suddenly as he stumbled over a little outdoor kitchen where a woman sat under a faded awning beside a charcoal stove. But she was good-natured and

"I See a Tall Boy—Yes, It Is You"

only cried, "Look where you're going, boy. Are you so hungry that you cannot see?"

"At least I can smell something good," answered Timon cheerfully, and untieing a small coin from the corner of his tunic, held it out for a small dish of porridge, flavored with shrimps and onion.

Then Timon hurried down the hill, past the public baths where, beyond the shady arcades and awnings, he could hear the splash of bathers and sound of their talk.

The factories and workshops were built near the waterfront, where they could easily reach both the market and the ships. The pottery shop was already open and buzzing with excitement, and Ambrose the overseer, quite red in the face, was ordering everyone around.

"Clean up those tables!" he told one workman. "Scratch all the clay off those boards," he said to another. "Timon, I am glad you are on time for once. Arrange the painted vases on the shelf nearest the doorway where the light is best, and see that you make them look their nicest. Today the master and some of his friends are coming to inspect the shop, and who knows when they may see fit to arrive!"

Timon liked arranging these picture vases, because they were beautiful and full of interest. They showed scenes from almost every kind of Grecian life. He was glad Ambrose hadn't told him to arrange the common pottery instead—such things as the large jugs and vases for storing oil and grain, the plain clay pitchers for carrying water, or even the small clay lamps and toys.

There were altogether nearly forty workmen, some of them out in the yard shaped and molded damp clay and water into shape and then baked it in the round ovens, so it would be hard. Afterwards, the finest ones would be glazed or painted.

When he had finished his share of the cleaning, Timon sat on a low bench beside a white-bearded old man who was one of the highest-paid artists, and the boy carefully mixed dry paint-powder, imported from the city of Tyre, with water in a bowl.

"Of late you are becoming quite skilful with the colors," said the old man, and Timon was pleased, for the artist was so proud of his fine vases, that when he had finished one, he signed it with his name (as artists today sign a picture).

"Every man go to his bench!" shouted Ambrose excitedly. "Here comes the master!" But after all it was a false alarm—another customer strolled in to look around.

Poor Ambrose nearly wore a path between the workbenches and the open doorway, but he needn't have worried so much, for the merchant owner didn't come till late. When the shadow of the column in the marketplace looked long and thin as a galley mast and stretched across nearly to their doorway, there was the sound of wheels and horses' hooves, and two chariots drew up at the door with a flourish.

Timon caught a glimpse of the splendid horses and the charioteers in long robes, and he stepped to the back of the shop where he could look on without being in the way.

Ambrose was bowing and smiling, as he lifted the curtain from the doorway and two men and a boy entered the shop, which seemed to brighten by the rich coloring of their clothes and jeweled ornaments.

The boy, whose short curly hair was held in place by a purple fillet, was especially fine, and suddenly Timon recognized him as the boy who had passed him in the street the other day and laughed so scornfully, and Timon felt his face grow hot and red with anger. "So he was the owner's son! Well, Timon liked him none the better for that!"

But Arius had not even noticed Timon. He was looking about with interest, admiring the finished pieces of pottery, and outside he heard the whir of a potter's wheel and could see a man throw a lump of wet clay, like dough, upon it, and turning the wheel with his foot, thrust his thumb into the center to hollow it, and skilfully shape a vase, which the turning wheel kept smooth and even. Spouts and handles must be added afterwards.

"My son wishes to choose a gift for his mother," Timon heard the owner saying. "It is a birthday gift because of the new baby in our home."

"Yes, master.—A son as fine as this your firstborn boy, I trust," said Ambrose, with a respectful bow to Arius.

At sound of these fine words, Timon felt his ears growing hotter. He was remembering the things he wanted to say to Arius, whom he imagined was conceited and spoiled.

"Which do you wish, young master?" asked Ambrose, rubbing his hands together.

Arius found it hard to choose between one of red clay, on which the figures of soldiers in crested helmets and carrying shields stood outlined in black, or another where "Neptune" was shown rising from the sea, riding on a dolphin and carrying his scepter—'trident.'

"These are both very nice, but I think I like best the one the artist is still making," he said at length.

This was a lively hunting-scene made in black on a bright yellow background, which shone with a glossy luster. There could be seen the running dogs (so important to hunters that the Greek word for a hunter was 'dog-puller'); the men throwing spears and javelins and driving the game into a big net. The artist turned the vase around so he could see the leaping animals of many kinds dashing into it, for these seemed to be unusually lucky hunters. "But unfortunately it is not yet finished, master," said the old man.

"Too bad, for it is the one I want," said Arius, who was used to having his own way about most things. "Can you finish it for me tonight?"

"Oh yes, our artist will stay after hours," promised Ambrose. "If the young master will be so kind as to send a slave for the vase sometime after dark. Here is an extra key so he can let himself into the shop. Be sure he is a trusted slave, I beg, for there are many valuable things in your father's workshop."

"I will come with him myself," said Arius, smiling, but Timon didn't listen any longer. He was feeling more irritated than ever. "Work overtime indeed! Just because the spoiled boy couldn't choose another vase," he thought.

The owner walked to the other side of the shop with Ambrose, but Arius, looking around, noticed Timon for the first time. "Who are you staring at, slave?" he demanded, stepping forward.

"I am not a slave," answered Timon indignantly, "and

if you weren't the owner's son, I'd certainly tell you what I think of you!"

"I'd like to see you try it," said Arius, who suspected these remarks would not be complimentary, and he motioned with his ringed hand toward the back door of the shop.

Timon followed him, but was astonished and he could hardly remember what he had wanted to say. "You're just a spoiled child who has nothing to do but wear fine clothes and order your father's servants about," he growled.

"I could get my father to throw you out of work for saying that!"

"I don't care if you could," answered Timon, angrier than ever. "You don't know what real work is and you couldn't even lift a vase full of water!"

"Is that so?" cried Arius, tearing off his fine cloak and pouncing on Timon. Not for nothing had Arius spent long hours each day in the gymnasium, and in an instant they were rolling over and over in the dusty street.

"What in the name of all the muses, is going on out here!" cried Ambrose excitedly, coming through the door, and— "Is that my son, Arius?" demanded his father, staring.

Both boys jumped to their feet, feeling rather foolish. Their clothes torn, their faces scratched and smeared with dust!

"Now my real troubles are just beginning," thought Timon, but instead of telling his father that he had been insulted, Arius only laughed and said, "We were just trying our strength. This fellow has never been to a gymnasium, but his muscles are good!"

Putting on his cloak, he turned away, and Timon was astonished to find himself beginning to like the rich boy.

CHAPTER VI

AT DEAD OF NIGHT

WHEN everyone else was ready to go home, the white-haired artist was still leaning over the vase he was making, putting on the finishing touches, but he didn't look tired. He was happy because all the figures were full of life and beauty.

"Good-bye!" called Timon, the last to leave the shop, and in a few swift steps he had reached the smithy.

"Well, well!" exclaimed Cosimo, the moment he entered the door, "What have you been up to now? You look as though you had been having a battle with the Minotaur or some such mythical monster."

He laughed heartily at Timon's face, as the boy remembered that his tunic was torn and covered with earth stains. "I have not been fighting any monster, good Cosimo. It was the owner's son. I told him he was nothing but a spoiled child and he was angry, so we had a quarrel."

"What?" roared Cosimo. "The owner's son! Better

a dozen Minotaurs! What do you think will become of your job, after this?"

"Really I couldn't help it!" explained Timon. "The fellow called me a stupid slave, but after all he could fight quite well, and when his father came, the boy didn't tell that we had quarreled."

"It seems to me that you were as much at fault as he," said the blacksmith, "and you're lucky if you don't get into serious trouble!"

Timon felt that he had been rather foolish and tried to put the whole matter out of his head, by taking the great hammer and making the anvil ring while he took his evening exercise.

"Where are the new sandals you were boasting that you would buy this morning?" asked Cosimo above the noise.

"I didn't get them, for I gave the silver plaything to an Egyptian, so she would tell my fortune," answered Timon, leaning on his hammer. "She was wonderful and seemed to know all about me, though we had never met before, and she said I would have some adventure today—though she did speak about the moon!"

"You shouldn't listen to fortune-tellers," said Cosimo, "unless perhaps to the voice of the oracle at Delphi. The poet Euripides said—'The best fortune-teller is he who guesses well,' and no doubt this woman could guess many things from looking at you and hearing what you said. The muscles in your arms might help her to guess you want to be an athlete. Well, we live and learn and perhaps the silver toy will have been of use to you, if it teaches you a lesson." Cosimo turned away and the matter was ended.

Soon after their simple meal, Timon threw himself down on the sheepskin in the corner and fell asleep. It was a warm night and the door of the smithy stood open, but already the narrow street was almost deserted. Timon slept for what seemed a long time but at length was awakened by the sound of voices and laughter outside, and the flare of torches, as a group of late merry-makers went on their way home from some party, for Corinth was a very gay city for those who had money.

Timon had no way of telling the time except he knew it was the part of night called "the dead hours." He stared out the door at the sky above the rooftops and saw the round, fat face of the moon looking down at him. Timon sat straight up in bed, for the moon was wearing a fillet of clouds around it.

"My adventure!" thought Timon, suddenly wide awake. "Of course it won't come to me if I lie here in the corner of the smithy." Quickly he rose to his feet and tiptoed to the door. There was no sound but the energetic snores of Cosimo and the squeak of a rat.

The street was once more silent and deserted. It looked so dark and mysterious that Timon felt excited little shivers run up his back. Most of the merchants had put boards across the fronts of their shops and those who had doors with keys, had locked them securely and were sleeping somewhere in the upper story.

Timon looked at the row of ghostly buildings, black and looming like giants standing guard till morning. Only one of them seemed to be awake and that was the familiar workshop of the pottery trader where a light was shining through the door cracks.

"That's queer," thought Timon. "Certainly the artist must have finished his vase long ago. I wonder if the boy Arius and his slave are there as late as this? I think I'll go and see, but I won't make any noise!"

As Timon stole quietly to the door, he could hear movements and rattling sounds inside and the low murmur of voices, and then a queer grunting sound which made the roots of his hair feel shivery.

It wouldn't have astonished Timon at all to see some frightful three-headed monster, such as Corinthian storytellers described, but he bravely stood his ground and peered in the crack. There he saw two burly men wrapped in long garments like charioteers. One was bending over a large basket, putting something inside it, and the other lifting the precious painted vases off the shelf and handing them to him.

On the floor there also lay two big bundles and while Timon stared with bulging eyes, one of the bundles moved a little and gave a queer grunt. Timon saw it was something wrapped in a fine embroidered cloak of gold and purple, all bound about with rope, but at one end showed a pair of feet wearing sandals.

It was Arius' cloak! Probably Arius' feet! He must have been captured by the wicked men. The other and bigger bundle now gave a heave like a giant caterpillar trying to get out of a cocoon, and one of the men kicked it.

Timon wasted no more time looking on, for it was plain these men were robbing the workshop, and goodness knows what they would do with poor Arius and the servant who was probably tied in the other bundle!

Darting back to the blacksmith shop on silent bare feet, Timon shook Cosimo by his great shoulder and said, "Wake up, wake up! Thieves are in my master's workshop and have captured his son Arius. We must go and save him."

Though only half awake, Cosimo quickly got the

He Bravely Stood His Ground

idea and, jumping up, grabbed the blacksmith hammer, while Timon armed himself with an iron bar.

"You go to the back door and yell," whispered Cosimo, "and I'll go in the front door and hit them over the head with the hammer. Don't try to fight unless you have to save yourself."

When the quiet of the workshop was broken by a horrible yell, the thieves dropped what they were holding and looked about for a way to escape. One of them dashed out the back door, tripping up Timon, who only managed to hit one of his feet with the bar as he was running away.

The other thief turned to the front door, upsetting a big vase, but when he saw Cosimo standing huge and dark, outlined against the sky, he thought it was Vulcan himself, come from Olympus to punish him, and with a cry of fear ducked under the blacksmith's great arm just in time to save himself a blow on the head with the hammer.

"Well, our men have escaped," said Cosimo, feeling a little disappointed. "But anyway, we saved Master Cyrus' treasures, all except this one that is broken!"

Timon was untying the ropes from around Arius, who sat up and rubbed his head. "Where did you come from?" he asked. "It was awful lying here and knowing they were stealing my father's things. The slave and I came early, but the other men were hiding near the door, and when we opened it, came in and took us by surprise—My head hurts worse than when you punched me this morning!" Arius smiled and rose stiffly. "Well anyway, thank you for saving me, and now I hope we'll always be friends!"

"I hope so too," said Timon, "but if it hadn't been for the fortune-teller, I wouldn't have come here, and if the little girl hadn't given me the silver wheel, I could not have paid the fortune-teller, so you see, Cosimo, such things are useful after all!"

"But if it hadn't been for me, you might have been lying there yourself," said Cosimo with a chuckle as he unfastened the ropes from around the slave, who sat up and pulled a rag out of his mouth. "They stuffed this in so I couldn't call for help," he explained, and he and Cosimo ran to the door to try and find the bad men, but they were nowhere in sight.

A watchman coming down the street wanted to know what was going on, but when Arius explained and said he was the owner's son, he let them lock the door and go away.

Next morning, the merchant Cyrus paid another visit to the workshop. "Where is the boy called Timon?" he asked, and when Timon came forward, he looked at him and laughed a little. "Oh, so it is you! First you quarrel with my son and then you save him! You are a brave boy. What would you like most in the world?"

"Kind sir, I want most to be a famous athlete," said Timon, truthfully.

"It is a worthy ambition, but something I'm afraid I cannot quite give you. However, perhaps I can help, by letting you go to the gymnasium with Arius each day, and there you will also learn other things which are useful."

Timon mumbled his thanks. "But my work here, Sir?" he said doubtfully. "I am an orphan and must earn money for food and clothes!"

"Of course. But I think I can arrange that with Ambrose.—Ambrose, come here. They say this boy is a good craftsman. Pay him more wages and let him have two or three hours off each day to go to school with my son Arius. Now, Timon, take me to the blacksmith shop of the good man who also helped to save my son and my fortune. I have a reward for him too."

It was a fat bag full of money, and after the generous merchant had driven away, Timon said to Cosimo, "What are you going to do with all that money? Will you build yourself a bigger shop and buy fine clothes, or will you buy yourself a slave or two and stop work altogether?"

"And grow fat and lazy!" exclaimed Cosimo, chuckling. "No indeed. What use have I for fine clothes and slaves; and this shop has suited me for twenty years and I hope will suit me for twenty more! Just you wait, my boy, and you will see that I'll make good use of the money."

Winking one eye, he walked to the back of the shop and, digging a hole in the floor, which was only made of hard earth, he buried the bag of money, all but a little, and carefully smoothed the ground over again. "But take this bit of money, Timon, and run to the market and buy me a flute. I have always wanted to play a flute ever since I was a boy and lived in the country where my father played one while we trod out the juice of the grapes! And take this to buy yourself a pair of sandals and a new linen tunic so you will look proper when you go to that school tomorrow!"

CHAPTER VII

WEAVING ADVENTURES

TIMON, of course, was very happy to be in the gymnasium but was astonished to find how much more there was to learn than just to be strong enough to swing a heavy blacksmith hammer.

At first he felt awkward among all the better-trained boys, but it wasn't long before he could wrestle as well as any boy in the school, throw the discus well, and when it came to pulling the great bow, his strong arms and accurate eye sent the arrow winging straight to the center of the target, which was a large wooden cock seated on a pedestal.

To tell the truth, at first Timon didn't much enjoy the study of books and arithmetic. "I'd rather spend these spare hours swimming in the bay or fishing with the sailors on the waterfront," he confided secretly to Arius, who was now his good friend.

But Timon soon found things grow more interesting the more you know about them, and could do much harder sums on the counting-frame than he had ever known before, and was enough of an artist to find it easy to scratch neat letters on his wax tablet, as soon as he knew the alphabet.

It wasn't surprising that Timon hadn't learned to read and write. Books were few in Corinth of those ancient times, and there were no such things as newspapers or magazines because everything had to be written slowly by hand.

Cosimo, though he knew many useful things, could not read nor write, but was interested in the things Timon had learned.

"Today," said Timon, "the master told us that the Phœnician people invented writing, long before the Greeks knew anything about it."

"That rival nation whose ships are as many upon the seas as those of Corinth!" exclaimed Cosimo indignantly. "I know we buy Tyrian purple dyes from them and perfumes for the temples, but if I had to go to them for my language, I wouldn't talk!"

Timon laughed. "Oh," he said, "we made it much better by adding more sounds." Taking a knife he had been sharpening, he scratched two letters on the ground. "Now those we call Alpha and Beta, the first two letters of the alphabet, but the Phœnicians called them 'Aleph' and 'Beth' which means 'house' and 'ox.' And see, here is the way I write my name."

Cosimo stared at the ground and rubbed his beard thoughtfully. "They look to me like the tricks of a fortune-teller," he said, "and I for one can do very well without them! But I hope you beat that boy Lucien at the long jump again."

"I leaped as far as he did," answered Timon contentedly, "and I won the running contest, faster than any of the others except Arius!"

Arius, in the court of his father's home, gave his little sister Althea a final push in the swing, so that her small sandaled feet nearly touched the tops of the porch roof. "There, that's enough for today," he said, laughing.

Their mother sat under the shade of the colonnade, embroidering the border of a dress, and inside the open doorway could be heard the busy hum of a spinning-wheel. Corinthian women who had servants liked to make their own cloth instead of buying it.

The baby, no longer wearing swaddling clothes, lay in his cradle kicking his bare legs and playing with a little clay rattle made in the shape of a soldier and filled with pebbles. "Timon made the rattle himself," said Arius. "Don't you think he's a very nice boy, mother?"

"Yes, indeed," she answered. "And if I were you, I'd ask

your father if you may take him with you to the theatre tomorrow. It is a holiday, and people will be coming from cities all around to see the play."

"May I go too?" asked Althea, swaying lower and lower as the swing came to a stop.

"Of course not, dear child. You know nice women and girls do not go, and I don't think you'd like it anyway. We will stay at home like Penelope and her maidens in the old story, while Ulysses went forth to seek adventure. That is the proper thing to do!"

"I suppose so," said Althea, "but sometimes I wish I had been a boy instead of a girl. Why do you suppose I wasn't?"

Her mother laughed. "I don't know. Human beings aren't supposed to decide such things. Somehow I think you are a nicer little girl than you would be a boy, and what would baby and I do without you to keep us company? Get your little clay dishes and make some play food for me, or we can pretend that we are the 'Three Fates,' you and I and Cora by her spinning wheel. They sit all day and spin and weave the pattern for the lives of men, and they have big shears with which to cut the thread short at any moment. Let's think what pattern we shall weave for Arius today."

Althea was so much interested in this game that she

no longer minded being a girl and waved her small hand cheerfully to Arius as he went out the gate to find Timon.

The theatre in ancient Greece was only held at certain times of the year, usually to celebrate some religious holiday, for religion in Greece was very cheerful.

The great theatre was built out on the hillside with only the blue sky for a roof. It was shaped like a gigantic bowl with seats cut out of the natural rock—hundreds and hundreds of seats—and while the crowds poured in through the entrance gates, Timon, Arius and his father climbed up the aisles to find a place which would be shady and have a breeze from the sea.

"Those marble seats in front which are shaped like thrones are meant for the magistrates and city rulers," said Arius to Timon. "I suppose my uncle is among them, though it's hard to see from here."

The hundreds of heads looked almost like stones on a beach, and Timon found it hard to realize each was a living, thinking person like himself. "Look, there comes the captain from the Acropolis fortress and many soldiers!" he nudged Arius and pointed. They could see the sunlight on the soldiers' spears as they stacked them at the entrance.

The father stopped many times to speak with friends, but they were seated in time to see the constables and men who were there to keep order marching in to the circular space at the foot of the seats in front of the raised stage.

The scene on the big stage represented a forest, but it wasn't half as beautiful as the background of Corinth's blue water and sky, the rocky headlands and gently moving sails of ships, as fine as anything painted on a valuable vase.

"The play is about to begin," whispered Arius' father. "It is a tragedy written by the poet Sophocles, and here comes the chief actor!"

A hush fell over the vast audience as a door at the back of the stage opened, and out came a curious-looking person dressed in splendid robes, a tall golden crown, and with a great mask covering his entire head. The expression on this mask was very fierce and gloomy, and it had an enormous wide-open mouth so the audience could hear the singing and speaking of the man inside. He represented a hero king of old, and to make him look still taller and more important, there was a great tuft of hair on top of his head and he wore shoes with soles eight inches thick.

There were really only three actors, but one man could take the part of many people by merely going off the stage to change his robe and mask.

Nowadays we would think these ugly masks quite

funny, but Timon and Arius were as serious and excited as the rest of the vast audience, for it was certainly a very sad play.

"In the days of your great-great-grandfather," said Arius' father, "actors did not have these fine painted masks, but smeared their faces with the juice of grapes and stuck leaves on them, so they would not look like ordinary men!"

Things went from bad to worse in the play. There were many battles and quarrels and half the people were supposed to have been killed, until at length one of the gods of Olympus was supposed to come down to "earth" to take a hand in the affairs of men and punish them for their sins.

The actor representing the god had been seated on a small upper stage amid cloth clouds, and now, while men hidden from sight rolled stones about on a metal disk to sound like thunder, he was lowered to the stage by a kind of machine. He was called the *deus ex machina*—"god in the machine."

When at last this tragic play had ended, the Greek chorus of fifty singers and dancers in beautiful swaying robes came into the orchestra space at the foot of the seats and danced solemnly, telling the thoughts and warnings of the poet Sophocles about the things in the play.

"After all," said Arius, "I suppose it is just as well that little Althea couldn't come. She would have been crying by this time, though of course I think it was very exciting!"

"That's so," said his father, "but now we can all cheer up, because there is going to be a comedy, which all say is very funny indeed!"

And sure enough, all the actors wore comical grinning masks and went about in heelless sloppy slippers or bare-footed, and their clothing was stuffed with pillows to make them look still more comical. They made many loud jokes, even mocking and making fun of important people of those days, and so when the great crowds of onlookers filed out of the theatre, nearly everyone was laughing heartily.

CHAPTER VIII

THE RACE OF THE LEAPING DOLPHIN

ONE day Timon said to Arius, "Why don't you spend the day with me along the waterfront? I could show you ever so many interesting things…"

"It would be nice for a change," agreed Arius. So they started out gaily one fine morning when the sea looked like painted blue and purple silk.

They walked along the narrow, crowded streets near the docks and warehouses, jostled by porters carrying loads and by workmen going to and fro about their business, but they enjoyed the smell of the sea mingled with that of tar and wood and even fishy smells.

"Let's stop and watch the boat-builders a while," said Arius.

They strolled into the big open shed where sturdy workmen in short tunics, each with one arm and shoulder bare, were swinging heavy mallets, pounding and hammering the framework of what was soon to be a large galley.

Another carpenter was shaping and polishing a big oar of hardwood, while other oars, still longer, stood behind him against the wall. Rudders and rowers' benches, and ropes and other parts of ships, lay about.

"Good day, friend Eustice," said Timon, who knew half the people along the waterfront. "I see this ship has been on a long journey!"

"Indeed it has," answered a man who was scraping barnacles off its hull, while other men were caulking its seams with oakum and tar.

The great ship was lying hauled up on the beach, its underside showing like the stomach of a whale.

"Those new ships they are building are like young people who have not yet made a trial of life," said Eustice with a chuckle. "They cannot be sure whether they are weak or strong. Now look at this brave old beauty. She has sailed the mysterious distant seas! What strange sights and foreign beaches that figurehead must have seen." He pointed up to the weather-beaten carving of the Greek goddess Minerva on the galley's bow. "Rightly was this ship named for the goddess of Wisdom. She went to trade with Carthage in distant Africa, and on to barbarian Iberia (Spain), where she traded for so much silver that even her anchor is made of it. And on the way home, she was chased by Phoenician pirates, so her captain says, and still she safely made the harbor of Corinth with all her stores of silver and ivory and ostrich feathers!"

The boys went on, stepping carefully over great fish-nets spread out to dry, while the owners untangled their salt-encrusted strands. They had walked miles by midday and were very hot.

"Let's sit in the shadow of this locked warehouse and eat our package of lunch and then go for a swim," said Timon. The warehouse smelt pleasantly of spices stored inside.

After eating, they took off their tunics and sandals and leaped into the bay. It was always warm in sunny Corinth, and no Grecian who had a strong, healthy body was ashamed to go about without clothing.

They were soon splashing and leaping like dolphins, and cutting through the calm water like swift "penti-conters," the narrow fifty-oared galleys used for speed. (In those days, no ships ever had machinery or steam.)

They dodged a fishing boat just in time to avoid being caught in its floating net, and Timon looked up just in time to see the looming hulk of a galley and heard the creak of its rudder and oars and slap of water against its sides. Through the dark openings higher up he could see the forms of rowers seated on their benches.

"Look out!" yelled the angry steersman from his

little tower-hut at the end of the boat. "We have no time to change our course and lose our strokes for two water-rats!"

This was true and made swimming in the harbor all the more exciting.

Quickly the boys dove and darted out of the way, for the Corinthian galleys often had three banks of oars, one above another. And as the upper oars had to be longer than those below, they all had to be handled with different strokes. Even the trained rowers needed a special captain on each deck to help them keep time by playing on a flute.

At last the boys climbed ashore, dripping and slippery as two dolphins. Wiping salt water from their eyes, they put on their clothes and went home.

One day, Timon managed to borrow a small boat from one of his many friends along the waterfront. He took charge of the sail, while Arius sat at the one steering oar, and they glided out across the harbor feeling like true adventurers.

"Let's steer for the war galleys near the harbor entrance," said Timon. "I've always wanted to see them close at hand!" said Timon.

These towering ships lay at anchor with furled sails. They were huge "triremes" with three banks of oars each, and could carry hundreds of soldiers when it was necessary to go to war in some foreign land. Along the sides hung great round shields, shining in the sunlight, and in the bow was a long sharp "ram" with which to run down and split enemy ships.

As the boys sailed past the stern, they could see its pattern of leaves and feathers, and in front, to show its name, was a figurehead which represented Neptune, god of the sea and special patron of Corinth, which was gazing seaward as though watchful for enemy ships.

A soldier leaning on the rail under a bright deck awning called jokingly, "Where are you taking your ship, my fine fellows? Out to sea to trade with distant Corsica or perhaps still further to the mysterious 'Tin Islands' on the edge of the unknown seas?"

It was there the Grecians thought the world ended, and none of them could guess that the barbarous "Tin Islands," where all they could get was this useful metal, would someday be called "the British Isles" and be ever so important and civilized.

"Someday we may go to the Tin Islands while you are still here doing nothing more than watching the harbor entrance," answered Timon boldly. And they laughed, as he turned his small sail to the wind and darted quickly away.

"Today at the barber-shop," said Arius, "my father heard exciting news. 'Tis said there has been more trouble with the rebellious colony Corcyra," (now called the island of Corfu). "Too bad they do not love Corinth, their own mother-country, as do the other colonies!"

"Look out!" yelled Timon, for they were nearing a jutting headland around which they could see an edge of white foam like the glittering teeth of the sea. "Better turn back!" Timon hauled at the sail, but a sudden puff of wind caught their little boat and landed them on the rocks. It flopped over, and the sail floated helplessly, while the boys scrambled free and up the bank.

"Alas! Our steering oar is broken and the front of the boat crushed. What will my kind friend say, and how will we get home tonight?"

"I don't know how we'll get home," said Arius, "but no doubt my father will pay for the damage. Here, help me drag the boat up out of the water. We really should have brought some fire from the sacred hearth in the temple at Corinth, to light in this new land, as other immigrants do to represent the life of Greece!"

Arius was not half as worried as Timon. He was more used to having things come out right for him, but Timon said crossly, "Do close your mouth before the sea-gulls fly into it. New land for Greece indeed! This is only a

"WHAT IF IT'S PART OF AN ENEMY FLEET?"

silly point of rocks… Oh look, there's a sail. It's a ship coming in from the open sea. Can you see its flag?"

"Not yet. But what if it's part of an enemy fleet from Corcyra!" cried Arius, standing up to shade his eyes with his hand.

Both boys were excited, but as it came nearer, with the wind filling its great sails, they could see by its build it was a broad-beamed trading-ship without oars.

"It flies the Corinthian flag," said Timon. "When it comes nearer, let's swim out to meet it. They may pick us up and take us home!"

They waited while the slow ship seemed to grow steadily bigger, then the boys jumped into the warm sea and with steady, even strokes swam toward it.

The keen-eyed sailors saw them and dropped a rope over the side. They had been at sea so long that they were anxious to talk to anyone from the home-land, and as the boys scrambled upon the salty, weather-stained decks, sailors in round wool caps, with sun-burned faces, crowded round asking questions.

"Who are you?" demanded the captain. "I thought we were saving two hardy adventurers, but I see you are only boys!" He laughed, but looked astonished when Arius answered.

"I am the son of Cyrus, trader of Corinth, and this is my good friend Timon."

The captain smiled and gave a short bow. "Master Cyrus is owner of this very ship, the 'Leaping Dolphin'," he said. "Did you not know that?"

"Oh yes," said Arius, "but I hadn't yet noticed the figure-head. The Leaping Dolphin—it is a nice name, isn't it, Timon?"

"Yes indeed," agreed Timon. "She should be a lucky ship." For in Greece, dolphins were thought to bring luck to fishermen, sailors, and merchants, and early in May there was a big festival called the Delphinia after the dolphins. This was to celebrate the coming of the warm sun to shine kindly upon the waters, ships, and sea-creatures—especially the dolphins.

Timon and Arius looked about them with interest. There was a funny little monkey seated on the railing, and they had seldom seen such an amusing animal. "What's that queer voice calling in a foreign language from within the cabin?" asked Arius.

"It's only a parrot from the shores of Africa," said the captain, laughing. "Amuse yourselves by looking around all you like, but we have work to do. —To the sails, men! That Tyrian trading-vessel will overtake us if we move like a tortoise!"

The Phœnicians and Greeks were great rivals upon the seas, and the famous island cities of Tyre and Sidon had for hundreds of years been independent states like Corinth. They were now under the rulership of Egypt.

"You are not yet expected in port, sir," said Timon, who always heard all the waterfront news of Corinth.

"So much the better. If we are early, we will be the first to place our wares in the market-place and will get the best prices. That's why we wanted to keep ahead of the ship from Tyre."

Now that Timon and Arius knew the ship was racing, they lost interest somewhat in the parrot, monkey, and strange foreign cargo piled in the great hold, where sailors were already dragging aside the coverings while others were climbing about the rigging, shouting to one another and adjusting the mighty sail to catch the most breeze.

They soon passed the anchored war galleys and sailed between fishing-boats, where the men hastily hauled at their nets and stared excitedly, ready to give up a day's fishing chances for this new excitement.

When they reached the docks of Corinth, women and children were already running from far and near to greet their husbands and fathers, while merchants eager to buy and porters eager for work crowded the shores.

Out splashed the rusty anchor and the sea-stained ropes tied the ship fast, while the square sail was drawn up with ropes as one would close a "Venetian blind" and an enormous balance scales hung from the yard-arm of the mast. Baskets and bales of linens and ivory, peacock-feathers, hunks of silver, and papyrus plants from Egypt with which to make paper were among the things weighed out on deck and sold to wealthy merchants who had hurried across the gang-plank.

"Greetings, Arius and Timon! How did you get here?" It was Arius' father who asked the question, but he scarcely took time to listen to their answers—he was so anxious for his ship's cargo to reach the market-place. The ship was far too crowded.

The sailors were scarcely given time to greet their families, though they had been away more than a year. Sea voyages were so slow in those days that sometimes brave Greeks who wanted to go all around the coast of Africa would go ashore at some lonely place and plant crops, so they could have food to gather on the return journey.

The market-place soon hummed with business and excitement. Under its shady colonnades and colored awnings, people bargained back and forth, and bankers—called "table merchants"—sat at their low tables changing money for those who wanted it.

Arius and Timon walked about, looking at everything, and Timon wished he had enough money to buy some of the interesting foreign souvenirs.

"Another sail!" cried someone, and the call was taken up all about, while everyone looked toward the harbor.

"It's the Tyrian ship coming in and now prices in the market will go down because the men want to sell their things quickly before the others come!" said Timon to his friend. "Here's the chance even for a poor boy like me to buy a few things!"

Arius' father and the captain of the Leaping Dolphin chuckled good-naturedly. "Well, let them come now. We already have a good start!"

"How interesting it is to belong to a great trading-city like Corinth!" exclaimed Arius.

CHAPTER IX

THE OLYMPIC GAMES

"GOOD news, Timon," called Cosimo, one evening when the boy came home. "I've been counting this money the good merchant gave me for helping save his son, and we have enough to go to Olympia!"

"What?" cried Timon, scarcely able to believe his ears. "Do you mean we are going to travel?"

"Yes, at last I shall have a chance to see the wonderful Olympic Games, and you shall go with me. All we need buy is a cloak and hat and pair of sandals each, and we can start tomorrow. It will be a long walk, but our muscles are strong and we can stop on the way to visit my father's family on his farm."

Olympia was in the southern state called Elis and was named for sacred Mt. Olympus, supposed home of the Gods. It was the only city in Greece that did not have a wall to protect it. For Olympia was thought sacred and respected by everyone, and when festival crowds traveled there even from other nations, they put aside all warlike thoughts and were at peace from the moment the "peace heralds" announced the good news that all might travel in safety.

As Timon and Cosimo trudged along the rough road, their flat-brimmed hats hanging on cords down their backs oftener than on their heads (only travelers and messengers wore hats in Greece), they talked of these things.

"Only true Greeks are allowed to take part in the sports, you know," said the blacksmith. "Only those who are free-born, have never been slaves, nor even committed a crime or been in prison! But anyone may come and watch, and I do not doubt there will be some even from the quarrelsome colony of Corcyra, for they too will want to be represented in the motherland! Do you remember the great games at Corinth, one year when you were scarcely taller than my knee?"

"I remember a little," answered Timon. "The harbors of Corinth were more than ever crowded with ships and every inn and private house filled to overflowing, but this is even more exciting, and I don't know how to thank you for taking me."

"Then don't try, my lad," said Cosimo cheerfully, "and look—there are the roofs of my father's village and gay crowds on the roadways. Why the holiday clothes, friends?" he called to a little group of people jogging along in an ox-cart.

"Have you forgotten this is the festival of Dionyssus, the God of fruitfulness, grapes, and merriment?" answered an old man, aiming a bunch of grapes at Cosimo's face, but the jolly blacksmith opened his mouth wide and caught them in it.

Cosimo's father and mother were happy to see them. "Just in time to help us celebrate," said the old man. "Come, join the procession to the temple hill."

Under a shed near the farmhouse stood many tall jugs full of grape-juice, and the countryside seemed filled with their scent of grapes, while, as Cosimo said, "I remember when I was a fat boy and used to tramp out the heaps of grapes into a pan with my big feet scrubbed clean, and then, as now, all the people's arms and legs were dyed with royal purple."

The jolliest part of the festival for Timon was a game in which he joined with the village boys and girls, jumping about on fat, greased wine-sacks (which were made of the skins of animals tied tightly at the holes where feet and neck had been). Timon was the last to stay balancing on top, and his prize: a great jar of olive-oil. "But we can't carry it with us to Olympia, so you had better keep it here for cooking your food," he said to Cosimo's mother. "I wonder if my friend Arius in the city has had as much fun as I?"

"I suppose so," said Cosimo. "There will be jolly processions and all the people will dress up in funny clothes and make many jokes and pranks!"

When they went on their way, it seemed as though half the world were going to Olympia. Roadways in Greece were very rough and rugged, and many people found it easier to travel by boat, in and out of the many beautiful little harbors and inlets which indented the land. But a chariot is not hard to drive on a rough road, though it only holds two people, and there were some small two-wheeled carts like chariots turned the other way about and with one seat, so the riders did not have to stand all the way. Others went on mules or horseback, and a great many on foot like Timon and Cosimo.

"It's a good thing we aren't particular where we sleep," said Cosimo as night drew near. "Here is a grassy, sheltered spot behind these rocks which will suit me better than any dirty, flea-infested inn. Besides, the inns are often the hiding-places of thieves, and I might lose my money-bag!"

"All right," said Timon, "and here comes a man selling food. I'll run out in the road and buy something for us to eat."

As the Grecians were hospitable people, many travelers stayed in the homes of friends overnight, or perhaps had been given a token, such as half a ring, to show that they had been sent by a friend to the man who had the other half.

Timon and Cosimo had never seen a finer sight than the city of Olympia decked with flags and banners, gay with booths and tents where traders sold flowers, foods, and fillets for the hair, and a hundred other things. There was music and laughter and many jugglers and entertainers.

"Every state has sent envoys and representatives who are the famous and wealthy men of their cities. See how they have erected their silken tents and even brought slaves to wait on them," said Cosimo, stepping back to make way for a splendid chariot to pass. "He was a wise ruler who long ago planned these games at Olympia to please the gods. Do you know the story, Timon?"

Timon did not. He had just thought of the Olympic Games as always having been part of Greek life. But Cosimo explained that many years ago, a ruling prince had decided that the endless wars between the Greek people of the Pelopenessus would bring about its ruin and destruction, and displease the Greek gods if it continued. So he planned that these great gatherings for sports should be held every four years. They were dedicated to the god Jupiter and the hero of mythology, the mighty strong Hercules, and orders went forth that for a while before and after the five days of the Olympic Games, all wars should stop.

All about the grounds of Olympia and in its sacred groves stood beautiful statues of the Gods, Goddesses, and athletes who had won victories in former games. For the Greeks even began to count their history dates from the first Olympic Games, as we begin with the birth of Christ. The year 776 B.C. they called the Year One.

"We must go to the 'stadium' first thing in the morning if we want a seat where we can see well," said Cosimo. So they went there just after dawn, taking a little lunch to eat later, and as Timon watched the dusty, jostling crowds which soon began pushing by thousands through the great gates, he forgot that he was thirsty and hot and said, "I'm glad we came early or we might have to stand like those other people!" As it was, before the sports began, someone was sitting on his feet, and another man eating a piece of melon leaned against Timon's shoulder. But nothing worried him, for this was like the beginning of a dream come true, and he remembered that all should be peaceful.

The great rows of stone seats were arranged something like those of a Greek theatre, and at length there came a loud blast from many trumpets of the heralds and the show began with a beautiful procession of all the envoys and rulers from different countries, soldiers on horseback (riding without saddles but only bright horse-blankets fastened around the horses' necks). The soldiers wore shining helmets with great crests of metal or feathers as though they had been splendid armored birds. The onlookers stood up and cheered each for his own state, and Timon and Cosimo yelled "Corinth, Corinth," until it was a wonder their throats didn't split.

The judges of the games had been trained in all the rules for ten months ahead of time and had taken solemn oaths in the temple, to be perfectly fair.

There followed all kinds of athletic contests: wrestling, throwing the 'discus' of iron and the javelin, and fencing with spears. There were foot-races and jumping and all the things they had been teaching the boys in the gymnasium, but at sight of the skill and power of these trained men, Timon's admiration knew no bounds and his throat was parched and dry from yelling and cheering, in which, of course, the rest of the vast crowd of onlookers joined eagerly.

The prizes for all these wonderful deeds were quite simple. Only a wreath of olive, ivy or laurel branches placed upon the victor's head, or perhaps an amphora vase of oil. But the men who won, and all their fellow-citizens and relatives, felt that no greater honor could come to the family or state, and afterwards, as Timon knew, they would be feasted and given first-place everywhere.

There were also competitions between different poets and musicians to see who had written the finest poetry or music, and the winners did not even receive wreaths to wear, though they were carried in triumph on the shoulders of the others while everyone cheered. However, these arts didn't interest Timon and Cosimo as much as the athletic sports.

"Have you heard that the prize for the best runner is a beautiful amphora vase filled with oil?" said a man who sat below Timon and Cosimo. "They say it is brought by Cyrus of Corinth, whose craftsmen are among the best in the country."

Timon nudged Cosimo. "Did you hear that. My own kind master must have brought one of the very vases I have seen in the workshop and this must mean that he and Arius are here today, though nobody could see them in such a crowd…"

Soon there came another surprise for Timon. The herald was making the announcement: "Running competition for beardless boys. All free-born Greeks twelve years or under who wish to compete, go to the tent at the end of the course!"

Cosimo gave Timon a shove. "Go ahead," he said. "You'd better try. I've heard you boast often enough that some day you would be an athlete and name me as your patron! Now's your chance!"

"But after watching all these great men, I don't feel so sure I'm really skilful after all," said Timon, humbly enough.

"Well, these are all boys and he who never tries can never succeed. Go on!"

So Timon jumped to his feet and, leaping across the people below—who started to complain but stopped when they saw where he was going—he ran to the tent.

Running was one of the most important sports because trained runners were necessary in ancient Greece. They carried the news from place to place and all kinds of important messages, because there were no real post-men, no mail service or telegraphs and telephones as there are today.

When Timon reached the tent, he was told to take off his clothes and his body was rubbed with oil to make the muscles limber.

"Why, how did you get here, Timon?" asked a well-known voice, and there was Arius also getting ready to run.

"We came by foot and started long ago," answered

Timon. "I suppose you came by horses or chariots and perhaps passed us on the road."

"Well, I am glad to see you," said Arius generously. "But after so much walking I'm afraid your muscles will be better than mine!"

"Perhaps not," answered Timon. "You have had more training in the gymnasium. Anyway, this is our chance to do our best for Corinth and I would rather you won than any of the others."

Beside them stood another boy, long-limbed and strong-looking. "You Corinthian boys had better make up your minds you will not win," he said, scowling rather fiercely. "I come from Corcyra and am called the best runner in my gymnasium!"

For, as Cosimo had said, even people from the enemy colony of Corcyra were anxious on this great occasion to make fame in the motherland.

"Get ready," ordered the starter, and all the boys crouched in a row behind a rope. The moment it dropped, they were off—running in a series of leaps as they had been taught to do—and Arius was ahead almost at once.

Timon hadn't much time to think—only of his life-long ambition to be an athlete—and while his heart thumped with excitement, he dashed on doggedly, hearing the footfalls of other boys and their heavy breathing close beside and behind him. "If I had the winged sandals of Mercury, the messenger of the Gods, I couldn't get ahead of Arius now," he thought, "but I might beat that Corcyran boy!"

Someone stumbled and fell. Timon saw him as they crowded past. It was Arius and he now had no chance of winning for he had hopelessly lost ground. Now it was up to Timon to win. "For the sake of Corinth!" he thought. Straining every muscle, his breath coming in jerky gasps, he leaped forward. One boy dropped behind, another and another—and with a final mighty effort, Timon stumbled across the finish line.

A great thunder of applause from the thousands of onlookers broke out like surf breaking on a beach! Could it be for him? It was! People were shouting "Corinth, Corinth!" and Arius, panting and dirty, was shaking him by the hand. "Here, put on my purple cloak. They are calling you to the victory stand!"

So Timon wore a laurel wreath and when they asked him whom he should name to share the honor, he shouted proudly, "Cosimo! Cosimo of Corinth, my best friend and stepfather!"

CHAPTER X

PEGASUS AND THE CHARIOT RACES

AFTER Timon had been awarded the prize for running, Arius' father called him to his side. "Tonight," he said, "you may come and stay with us in our Corinthian tents. There will be feasting and fun and servants to wait on you and on your patron, good Cosimo the blacksmith. My family will be proud to entertain a true Corinthian athlete."

It is easy to imagine how pleased and proud these kind words made Timon, and it was wonderful to live in such comfort and luxury for the rest of the time they were in Olympia.

The Olympic Games lasted five days. The first and last days were used for religious sacrifices, processions, and banquets, but on the next to the last were to be held deeds of horsemanship and chariot races, and the crowds would all gather at the huge place called the hippodrome.

"My father has brought his chariot and two of his finest horses," said Arius. "Let's go to the place where they are stabled and I will show you."

"May I go too?" said Althea. Though it wasn't thought the proper thing for girls and ladies to sit and watch the athletic games, still they could enjoy the fair and all the surrounding fun and join in the processions, so Arius' whole family were here.

"My father has given me one of the horses for my own," Althea told Timon. "See, here he is. I have named him Pegasus after the winged horse of mythology who did such wonderful things with the prince Belerophon of Corinth. You remember how it is said they killed the wicked Chimera (half lion, part goat, and part dragon)…"

Timon knew the story, for Pegasus was supposed to have been caught and tamed by Minerva, the goddess of Wisdom, who gave him to Belerophon.

Althea stood on tiptoe to smooth her horse's silky arched neck. There were several grooms who had been brought to take care of the horses, and the charioteer who stood nearby said admiringly, "He would be beautiful enough even if he could not race… but just wait until you see those silken sides moving over muscles like steel. It is like the wind ruffling the surface of the Mediterranean Sea. — And we mustn't forget to praise

Hesper, who is named for the evening star and is black as a velvet curtain."

The charioteer wore a fine embroidered robe. He would drive the powerful horses in the name of the owner, his master.

At the hippodrome that day, Timon and Cosimo sat with Arius' family in some of the best seats near the front. They could easily see the fine performances among which certain soldiers competed — running to leap into swiftly moving chariots, fencing with heavy spears, leaping onto their riding horses straight up from the ground. These Greek horse-soldiers were called hippoltes, and the brave "Spartans" won most of the military contests.

"Now the chariot-race is about to begin!" announced the heralds.

There they were, lining up in their stands at the beginning of the course, which was a kind of semi-circle. Arius and Timon tried to keep their eyes at once on the restless horses and gleaming chariots and on a bronze dolphin resting on a high place at the beginning of the course. At the other end of the course was built an altar on which rested a great eagle.

At the signal — a blast from the trumpets — the bronze dolphin fell from its stand and at the same instant the eagle was set free and soared up over the altar. The ropes were dropped from in front of the chariots and the horses dashed off. They must go down the course and, turning, come back the other side.

They came thundering past, and halfway down the course, one chariot lost a wheel and tipped over. Two others got their wheels locked together and had to slow down while all the others whirled past. "I'm so glad it wasn't our chariot!" cried Arius, and they stood up to cheer as it dashed past. It wasn't hard to imagine Pegasus and Hesper really had wings and were flying, and as they drew near the goal in lead of all the rest, the crowd cheered again and again.

Pegasus and Hesper, prancing as though they were not in the least tired, drew the chariot up before the judges' stand, and the proud charioteer had a wooden fillet placed upon his head as a token that his good driving had helped win the victory.

But the real honor went to the owners — Althea and her father. The little girl was crowned with an ivy wreath and handed a palm-branch almost as tall as herself. And now the games were over, and the triumphal procession of victors marched around the altar to the sound of music and chanted victory songs such as Hail the Conquering Hero Comes — some of which had been written specially by famous poets for this very occasion.

When they started homeward, the crowds were pouring out of the city of Olympia like water over a dam, and Timon and Cosimo were grateful to be traveling in one of the carts with Arius' family and their tents.

Everywhere they stopped, people came to admire and praise the fine horses, who were now worth their weight in gold. And Timon also was given his full share of praise for winning the foot-race, and his heart was full of gladness. He had won the first step in his ambition to be a real athlete.

"Now," said Cosimo, "we can perhaps even out-talk the old soldier with our adventures, and hold our own back in the smithy!"

"And certainly there is no land so fair and fine as Greece!" said Althea, looking about contentedly.

"Yes — and no part of Greece so fine as Corinth," said Arius, "and we have three victors with us to help prove it," he added generously. "Timon, Pegasus, and Hesper! I am glad I am a Corinthian."

www.ingramcontent.com/pod-product-compliance
Lightning Source LLC
Chambersburg PA
CBHW021337060726
47591CB00006B/2064